Jon Scieszka's TRUCKTOWN on Reading Street

A BIG DENT

PEARSON

Glenview, Illinois • Boston, Massachusetts • Chandler, Arizona
Shoreview, Minnesota • Upper Saddle River, New Jersey

"Look at that dent," said Gabriella.

"It is a mess!

What did it?"

"A truck did it!" said Gabriella.

"It bent the hut."

"But what truck?" said Melvin.

"I can not tell yet," said Gabriella.

"It left a blue hint.

The hint will help us."

"It was a blue truck!" said Melvin.

"Dan? Ted? Max? Big Rig?"

"Look. Melvin!" said Gabriella
"The next hint is big.
It can tell us a lot!"

"Yes, that hint is big!" said Melvin.

"Just one truck can do that!"

"Big Rig!" yell Melvin and Gabriella.